P9-CSC-668

Don't Talk to Strangers!

BY Christine Mehlhaff
Illustrated by Kathi Ember

SCHOLASTIC INC.

New York   Toronto   London   Auckland   Sydney
Mexico City   New Delhi   Hong Kong   Buenos Aires

For Mom and Dad, with love
—C.M.

For my mom, Theresa, and my big brother, Steve
—K.E.

No part of this publication may be reproduced, stored in a retrieval system, or transmitted in any form or by any means, electronic, mechanical, photocopying, recording, or otherwise, without written permission of the publisher.
For information regarding permission, write to Scholastic Inc., Attention: Permissions Department, 557 Broadway, New York, NY 10012

ISBN-13: 978-0-545-00103-8
ISBN-10: 0-545-00103-X

Text copyright © 2007 Christine Mehlhaff
Illustrations copyright © 2007 Kathi Ember

All rights reserved. Published by Scholastic Inc.
SCHOLASTIC and associated logos are trademarks and/or registered trademarks of Scholastic Inc.

16 15 14   11 12/0

Printed in the U.S.A.
First printing, September 2007

Emma Lion loves to make new friends, but Mama told her to be careful and never talk to strangers. It's hard to follow Mama's rule because Emma sees new people to meet and talk to everywhere she goes. How will Emma know who is a stranger?

Brrrinnng! The phone rings as Emma and her big brother, Matthew, are eating breakfast before school. Emma loves to answer the telephone, but Mama answers it before she has a chance.

"That could be a stranger on the phone," says Matthew. "It could?" asks Emma.

"Yes," says Matthew, "and you should never tell a stranger where you live or if you're home alone."

"But how will I know if the person on the phone is a stranger?" asks Emma.

"A stranger is someone you don't know," explains Matthew. "If you answer the phone and you don't know who it is, tell Mama, or just say good-bye and hang up."

"Time for school!" calls Mama. Emma and Matthew put on their coats and backpacks. As they head for the door, the doorbell rings. *Ding-dong!*

Emma loves visitors! "Can I get the door?" she asks. But Mama has already opened it.

"A stranger could be at the door," warns Matthew.

"Really?" asks Emma.

"Yes," explains Matthew. "That's why you should never answer the door unless Mama says it's OK."

Emma and Matthew wave good-bye to their mother as they walk to the bus stop.

"I can't wait to ride the bus!" Emma exclaims.

"Riding the bus is fun, but just remember, you should never talk to a stranger at the bus stop."

"But how will I know if that person is a stranger?" asks Emma.

"A stranger is someone you don't know," explains Matthew. "If a stranger tries to talk to you at the bus stop, run home and tell Mama. Or tell a grown-up you trust, like a neighbor or a police officer."

"School was so much fun today!" exclaims Emma when she meets Matthew after school. "Did you have fun, too?"

Just as Matthew begins to answer, a car pulls up and Mrs. Giraffe asks, "Would you cubs like a ride home?"

"No, thank you," says Matthew. "We're taking the school bus."

"OK," says Mrs. Giraffe as she pulls away in her car.

"You should never get in a car with a stranger," Matthew says to Emma.

"But I know Mrs. Giraffe," Emma protests.

"That's true," says Matthew, "but we shouldn't take a ride from anyone when Mama has not told us to."

When Emma and Matthew finish their after-school snack, Matthew turns on the computer and opens up his e-mail.

Emma peers over Matthew's shoulder to see who has written to him.

"A stranger can find you on the Internet," Matthew cautions. "You have to be really careful about who you talk to. And if you ever get an e-mail from a stranger, you should tell Mama or Papa right away. Never reply to it!"

Emma is so excited to ride her shiny red bike. She can't strap on her helmet fast enough. Once Mama and Matthew both have their helmets on, too, the Lions zip and zoom their way to the park! *Whee!*

When they finish parking their bicycles, Matthew says, "You might meet a stranger when you're out riding your bike. You should never stop to talk to anyone you don't know."

"What should I do?" asks Emma.

"Ride straight home and tell Mama or Papa. Or if you see a police officer, you can tell him right away."

Emma and Matthew play in the park all afternoon. Emma is having so much fun! As Matthew pushes her on the swing, Emma asks, "Are there strangers here?"

"There might be. A stranger could be sitting on a park bench, or running on the trail, or playing with a puppy in the grass," explains Matthew.

"A puppy?" Emma shouts. Emma loves puppies!

"Yes," says Matthew. "But remember to always ask Mama for permission before you play with anyone's puppy, even if you know the person."

After the Lions return home from the park, Mama asks Emma and Matthew to go food shopping with her.

"Stay with us," Mama cautions Emma. "There are strangers in the supermarket."

"Emma," says Matthew, "a stranger might ask you for help, but you shouldn't talk or go with them."

"Should I find Mama then?" asks Emma.

"Yes, that's right," says Matthew.

As the Lions leave the supermarket, Mama has a surprise. She has bought the children candy. *Yum!*

Emma immediately unwraps the treat. It is her favorite! As she begins to take a bite, Matthew says, "There's a chance that a stranger might try to give you candy, but you should never take it from someone you don't know."

"Even if it is the peanut butter kind—my favorite?" asks Emma.

"Even if it is your favorite," says Matthew. "You should just say 'No, thank you!' and walk away."

"That would be hard—to say no to my favorite candy!" says Emma.

"Yes," agrees Matthew. "It would be. But it is more important to be safe!"

At home, Emma has a very important question to ask her big brother. "Matthew?" she begins. "How will I remember all these things about strangers?"

"It's easy. Whenever someone you don't know comes over to you, just stop and find Mama or Papa, your teacher, a neighbor you trust, or a police officer. They can help you," Matthew says.

"Can I find you?" asks Emma.

"Of course!" answers Matthew.

"And I can help you, too," Emma smiles, "because now I know what a stranger is."

Don't talk to strangers! But do talk to your parents or a trusted adult. If a stranger tries to talk to you, give you something, or take you somewhere, it is important that you tell someone.